The MOUNTAIN and the GOAT

Siamak Taghaddos

Illustrated by Amélie Touchet

I ran and I ran
Until a mountain appeared.

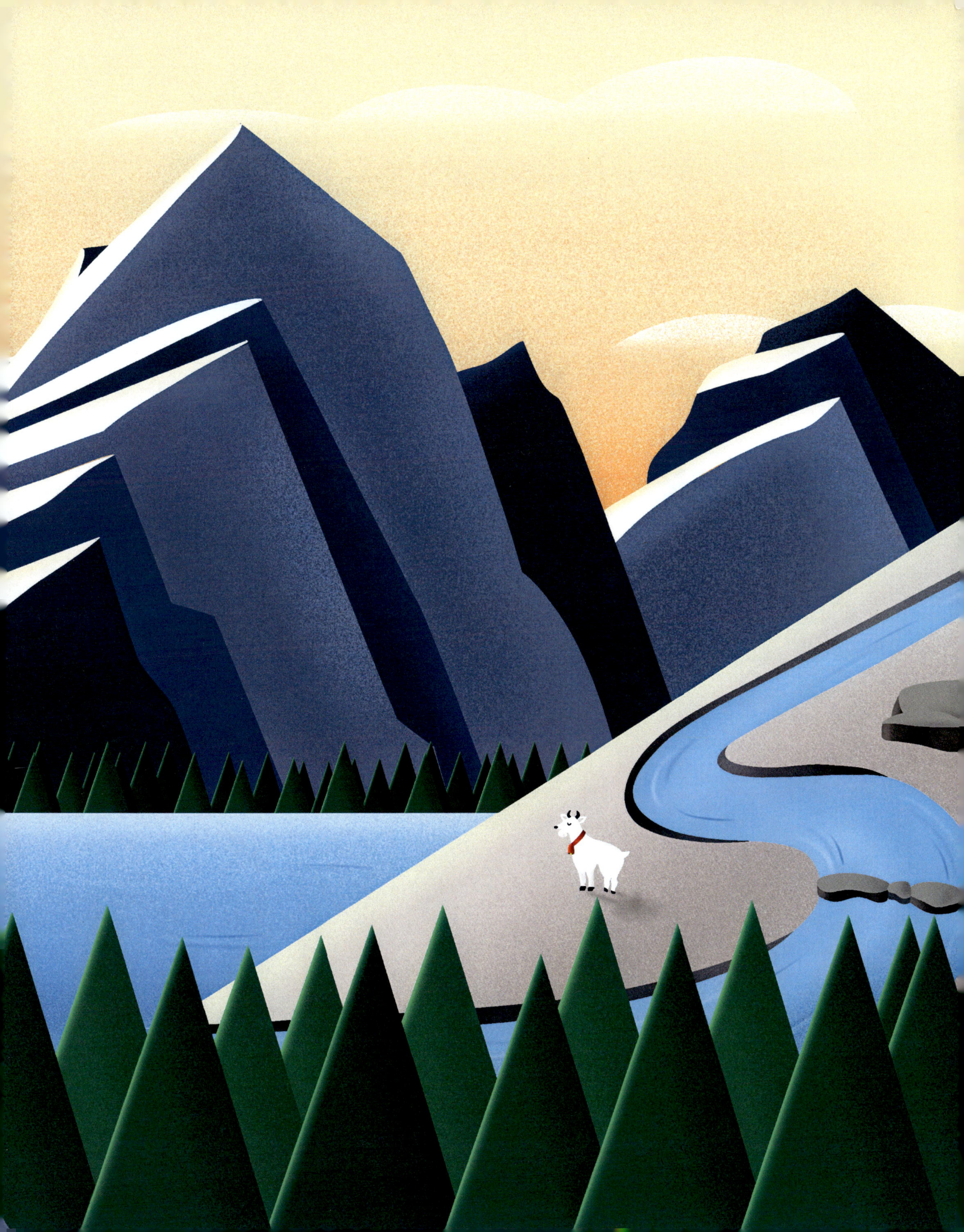

There stood a goat
Who smiled and cheered…

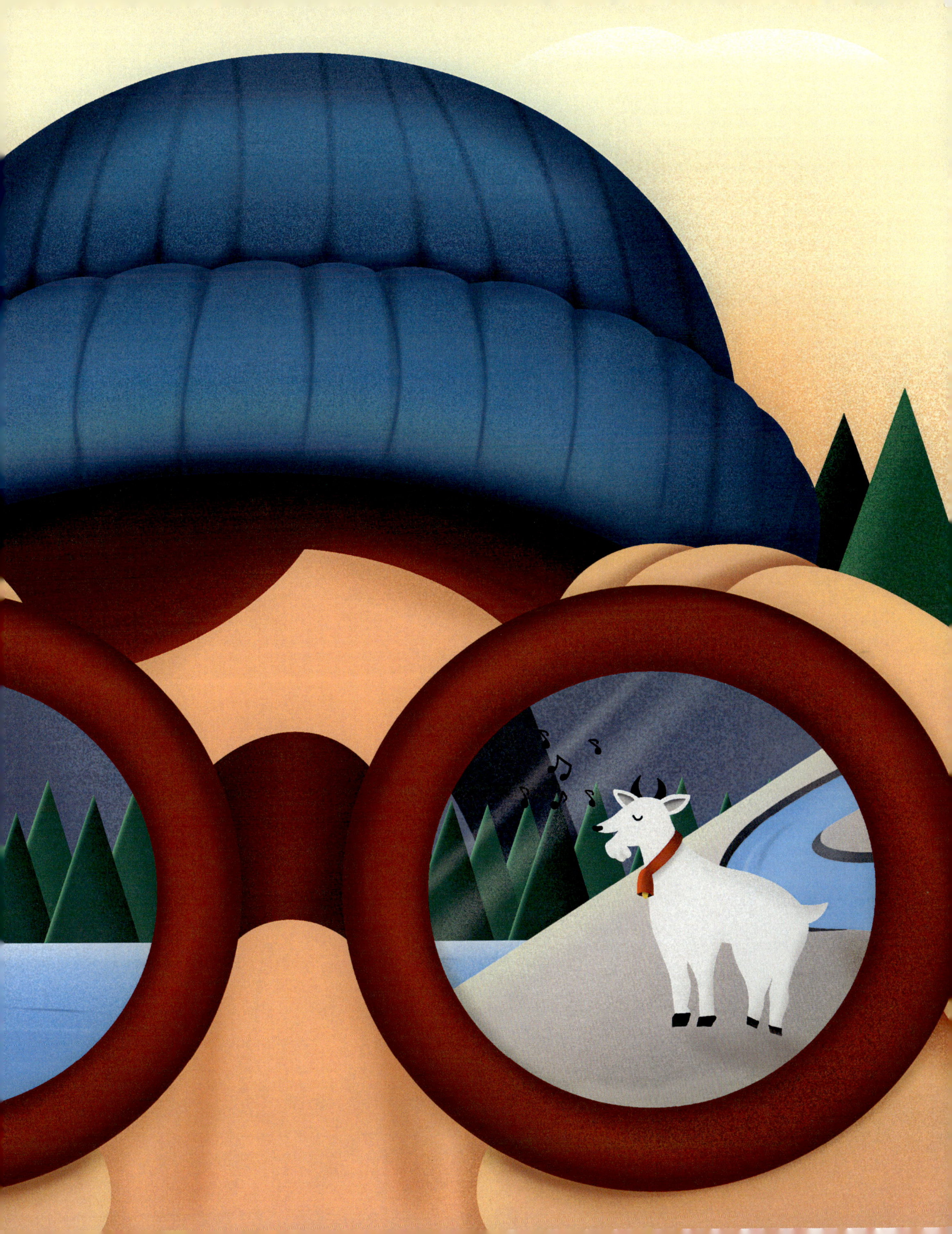

"Here's some bread,
And water too.
Use them well,
It's up to you!"

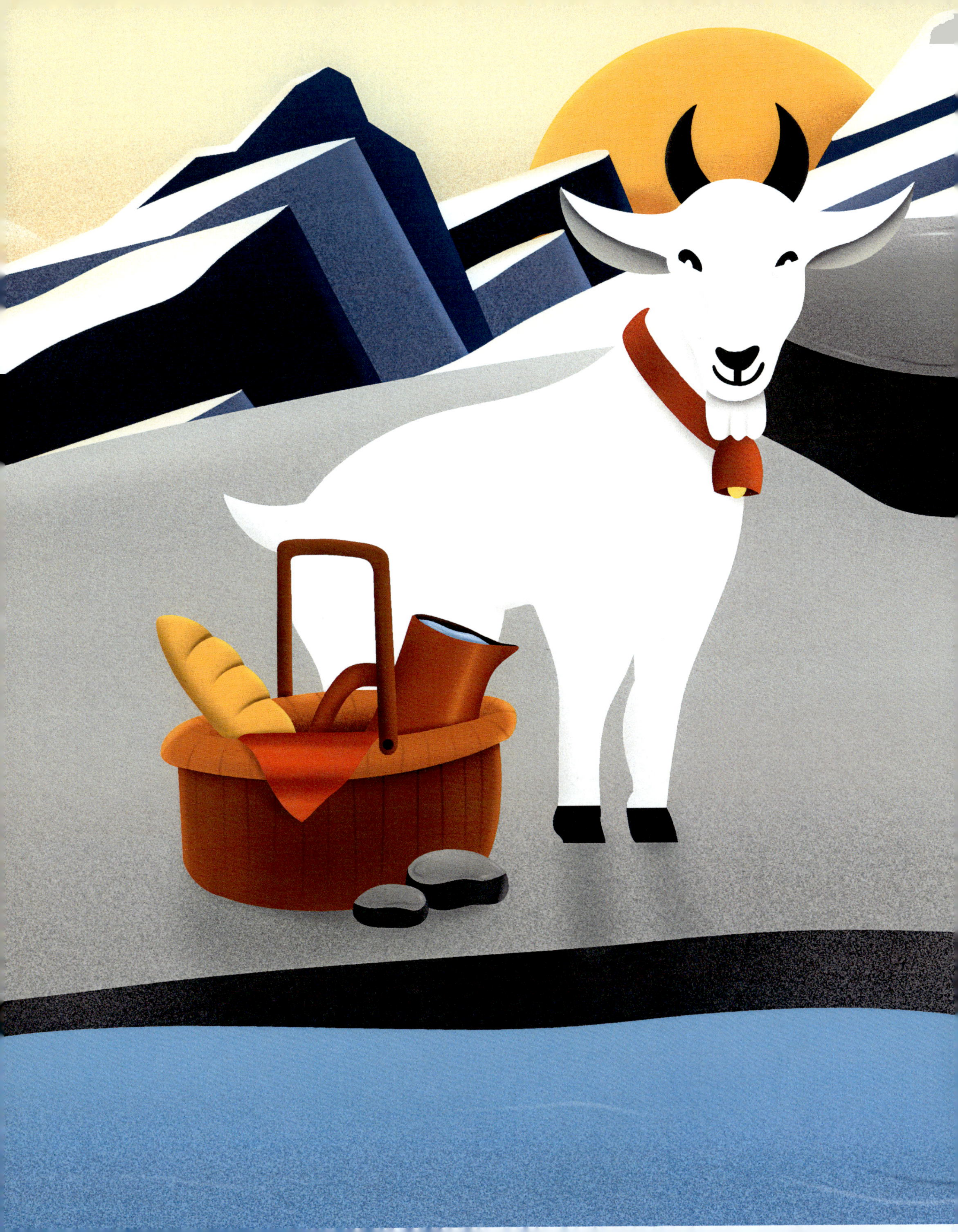

So the bread I ate,
And the water I poured
Onto the soil
Where grass could grow.

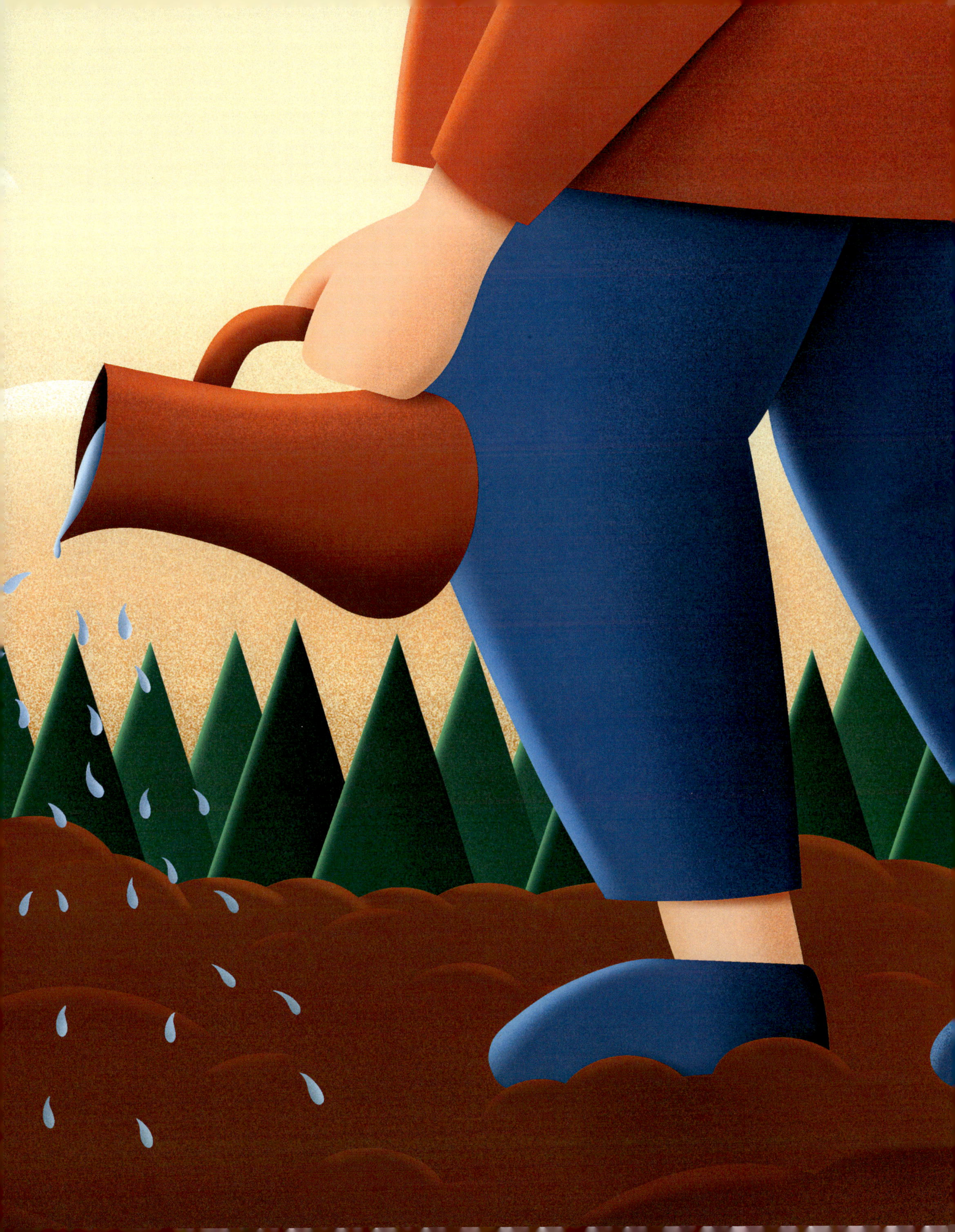

Soon the grass grew,
Green and sweet.

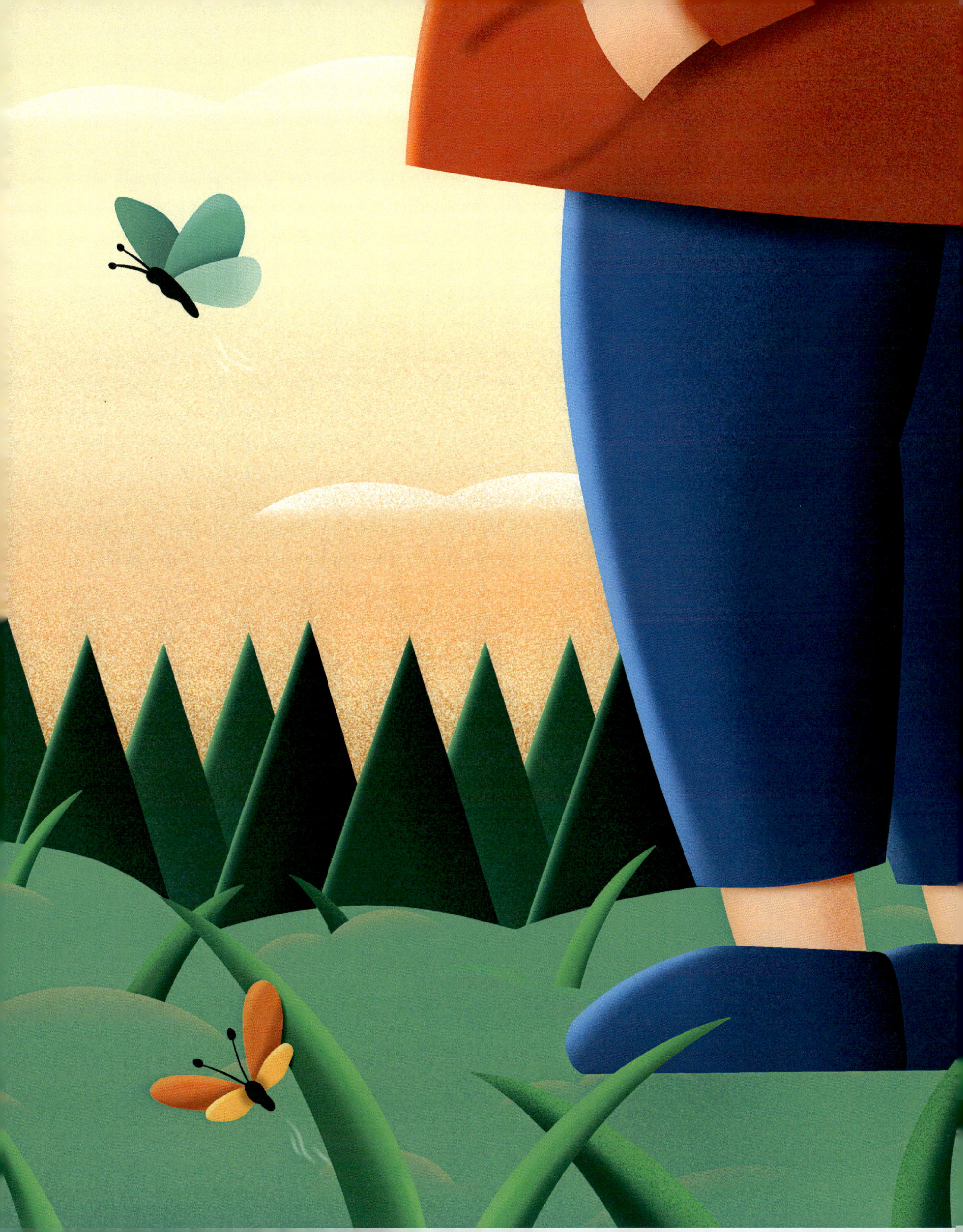

I bundled it up
For a cow to eat.

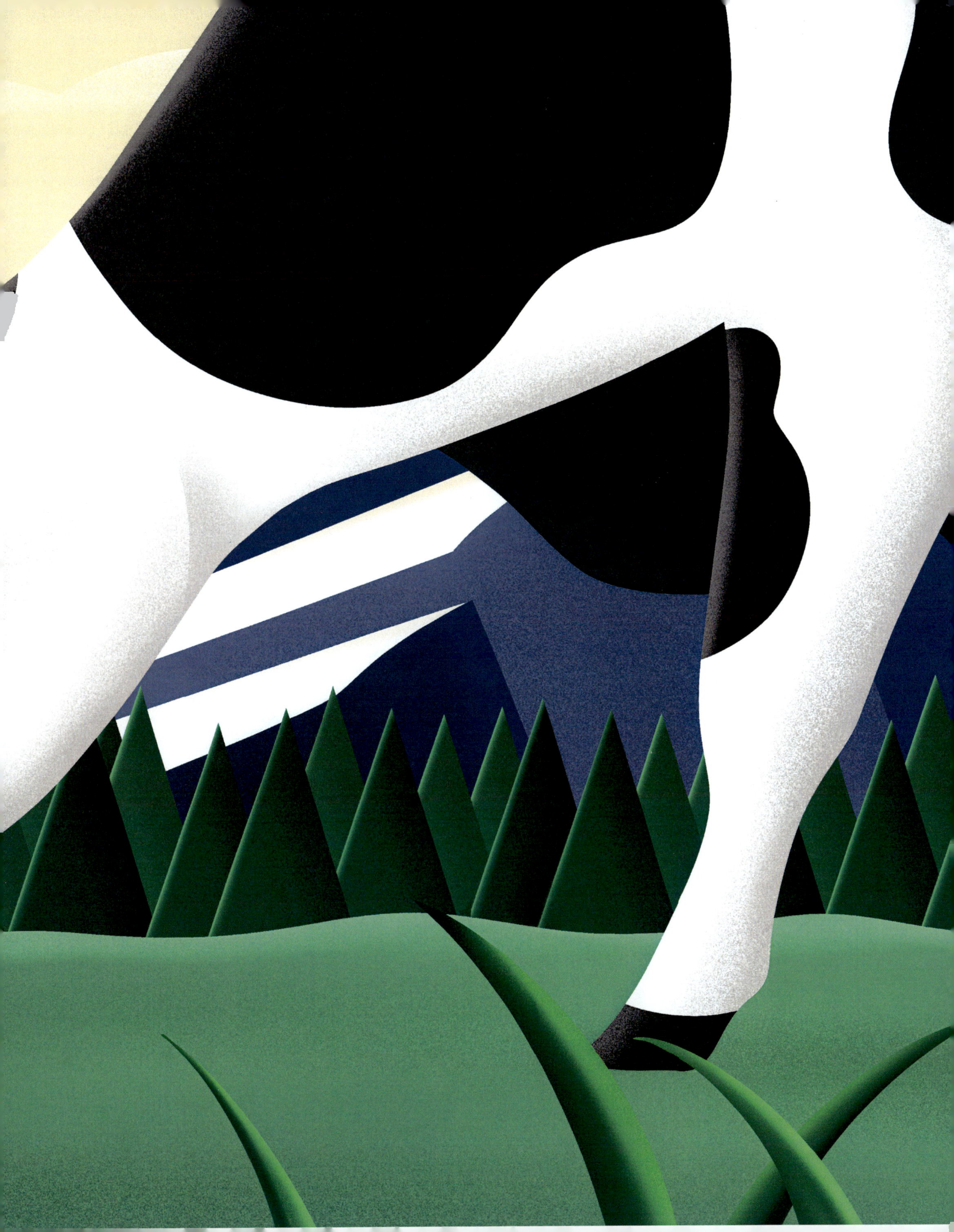

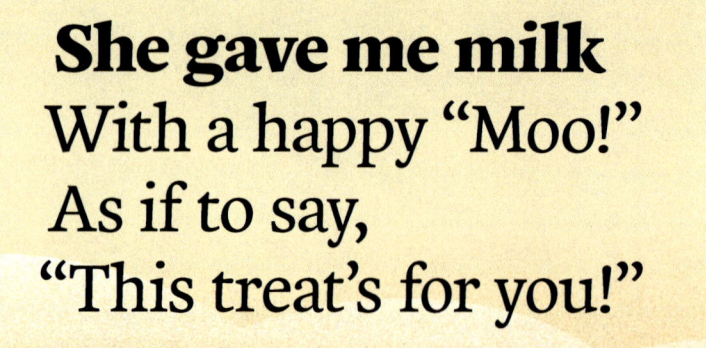

She gave me milk
With a happy "Moo!"
As if to say,
"This treat's for you!"

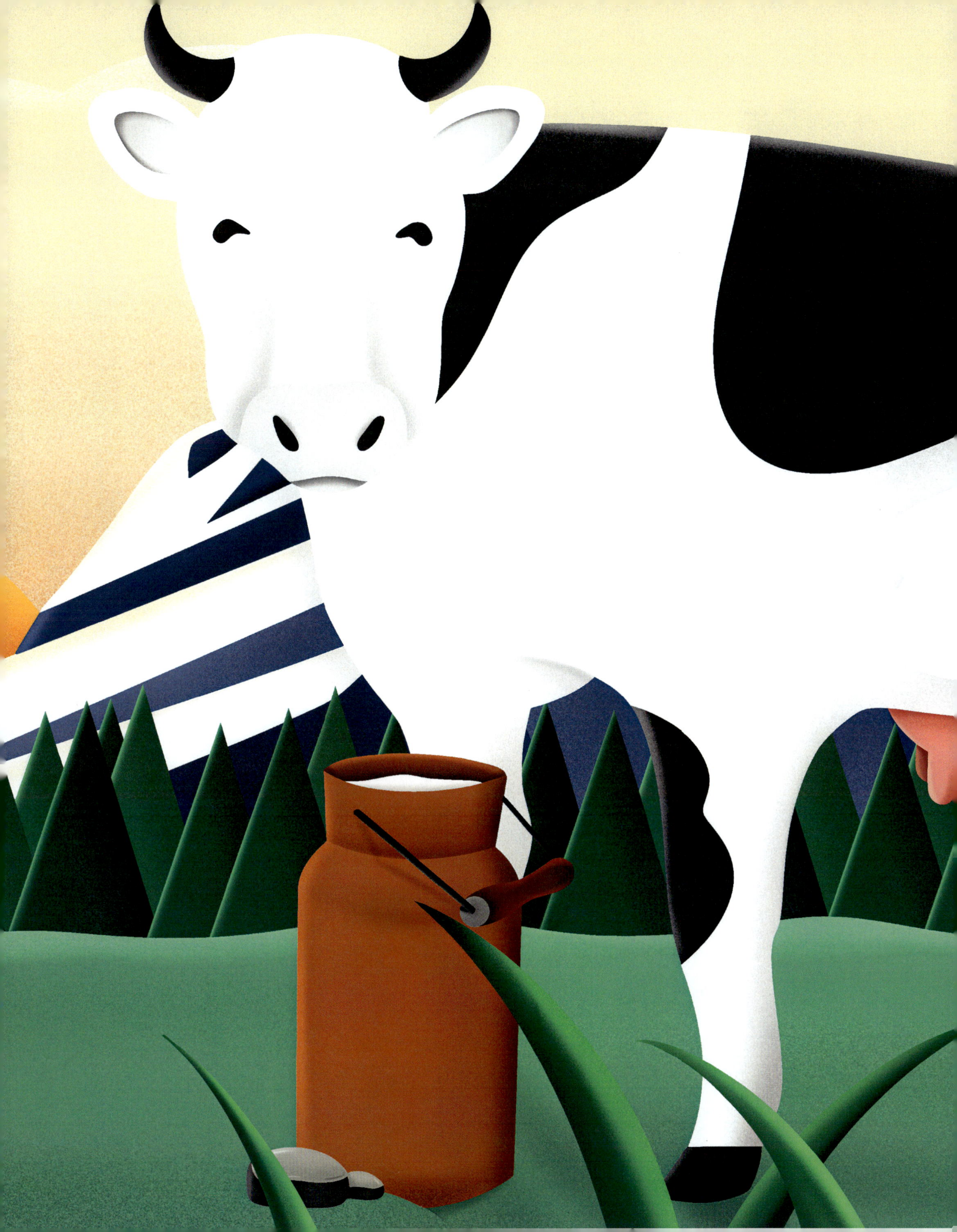

I brought the milk
To the smith with a beard.
He took a big sip
Then gave a loud cheer…

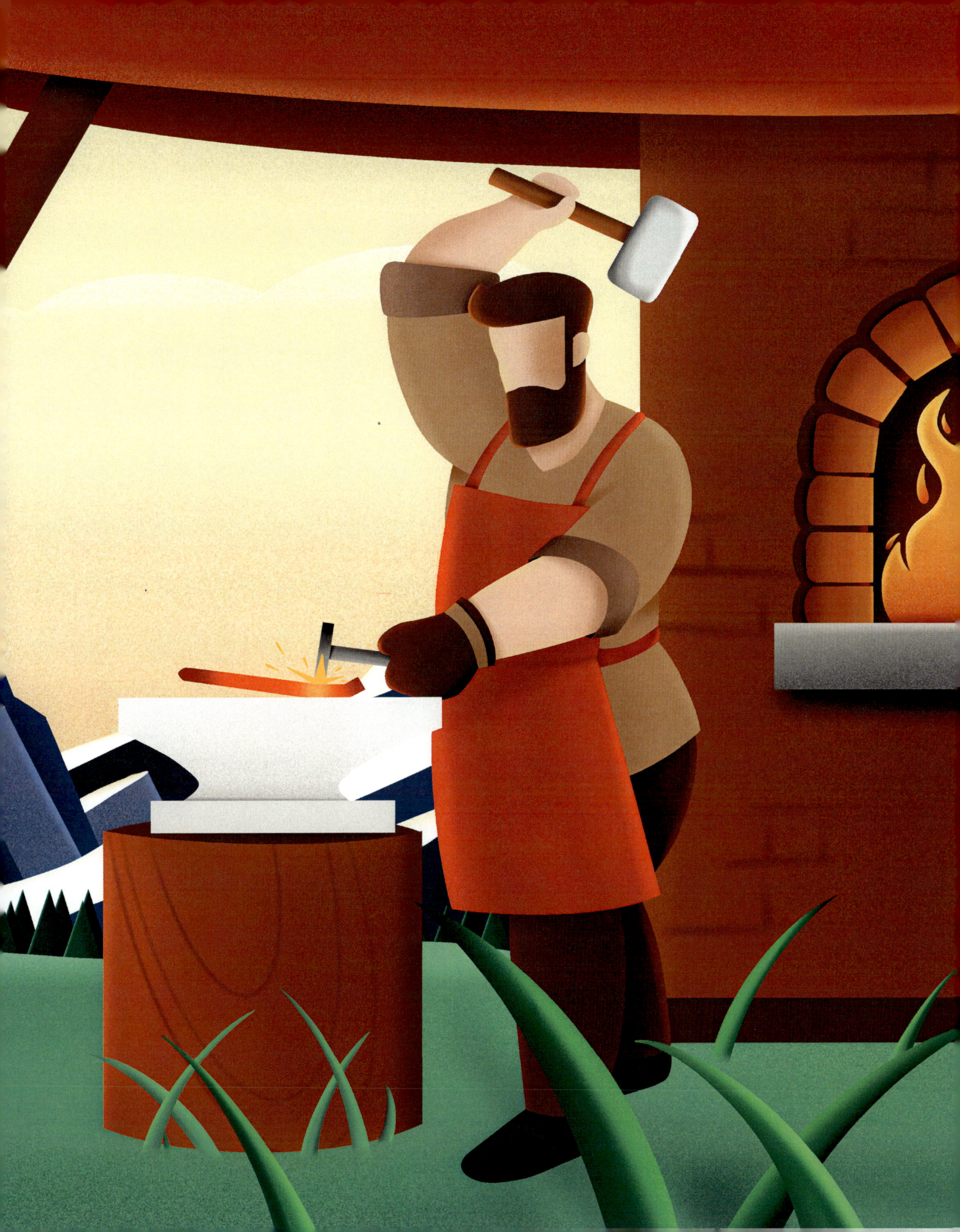

"This milk is so fresh,
Just what I need!
Take these new scissors
For your generous deed."

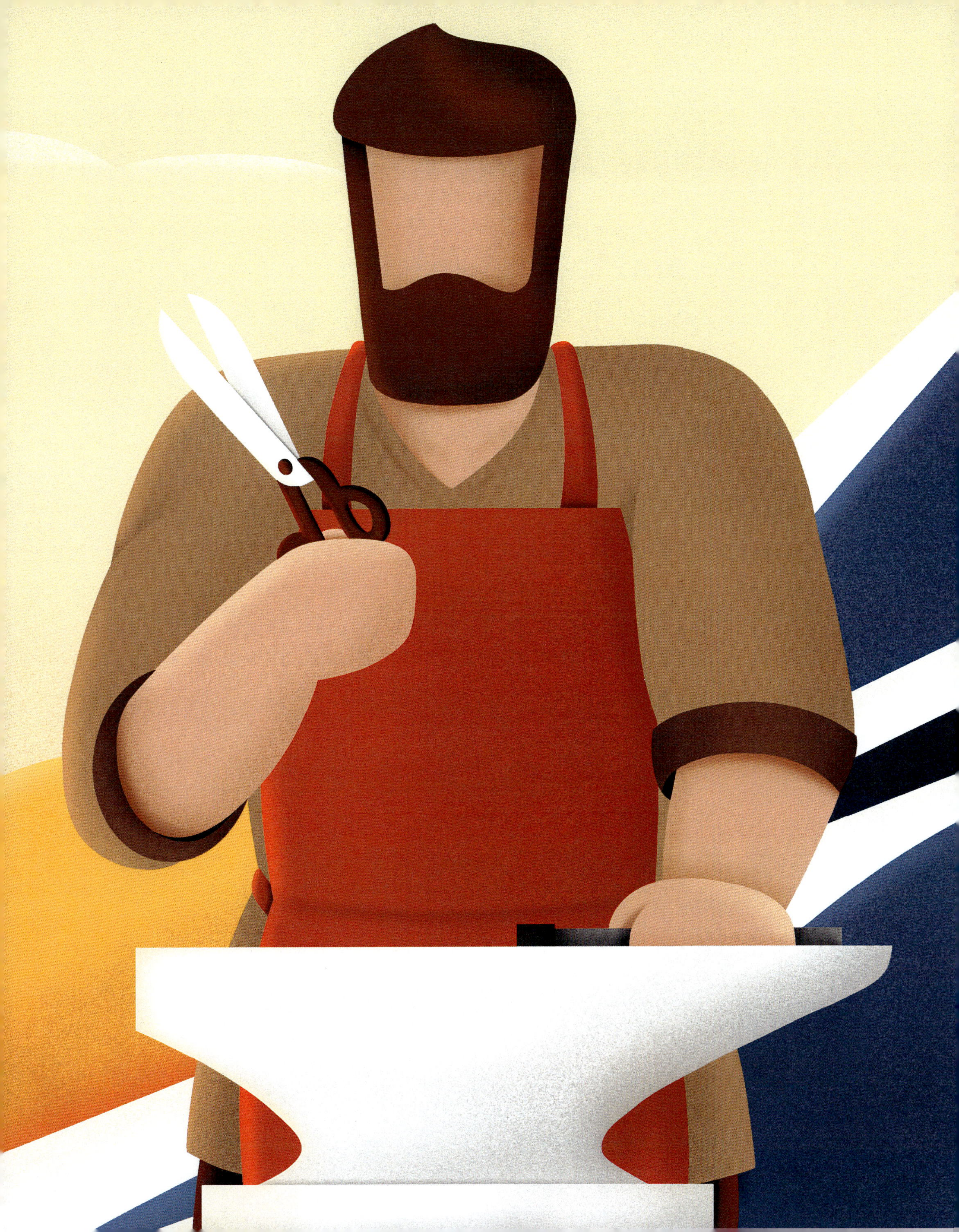

I went to the tailor,
Who was sewing a patch.
I gave him the scissors
And he said, "What a match!"

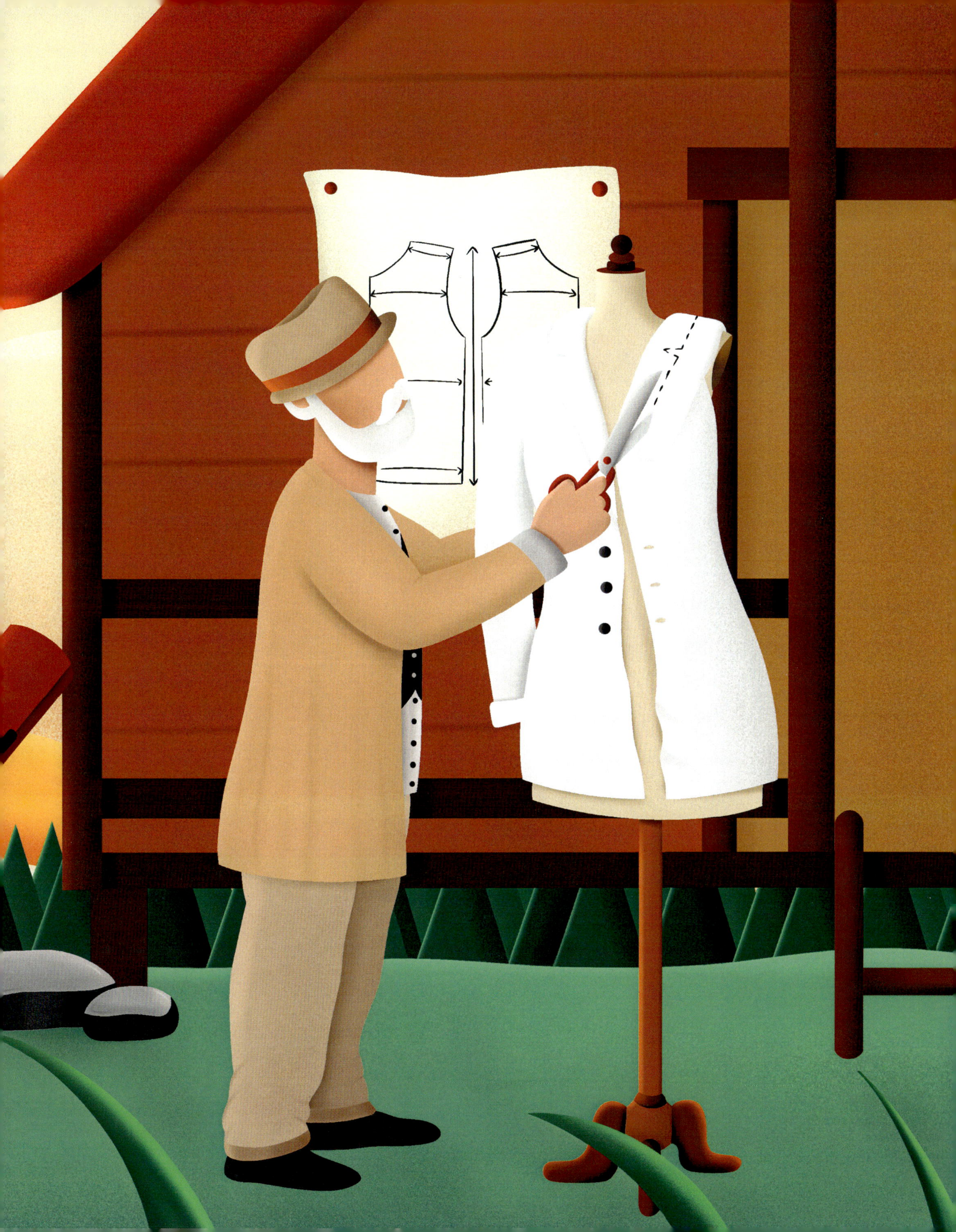

"Mine are dull,
But these cut true!"
He snipped and smiled
Then gave me a white coat,
crisp and new.

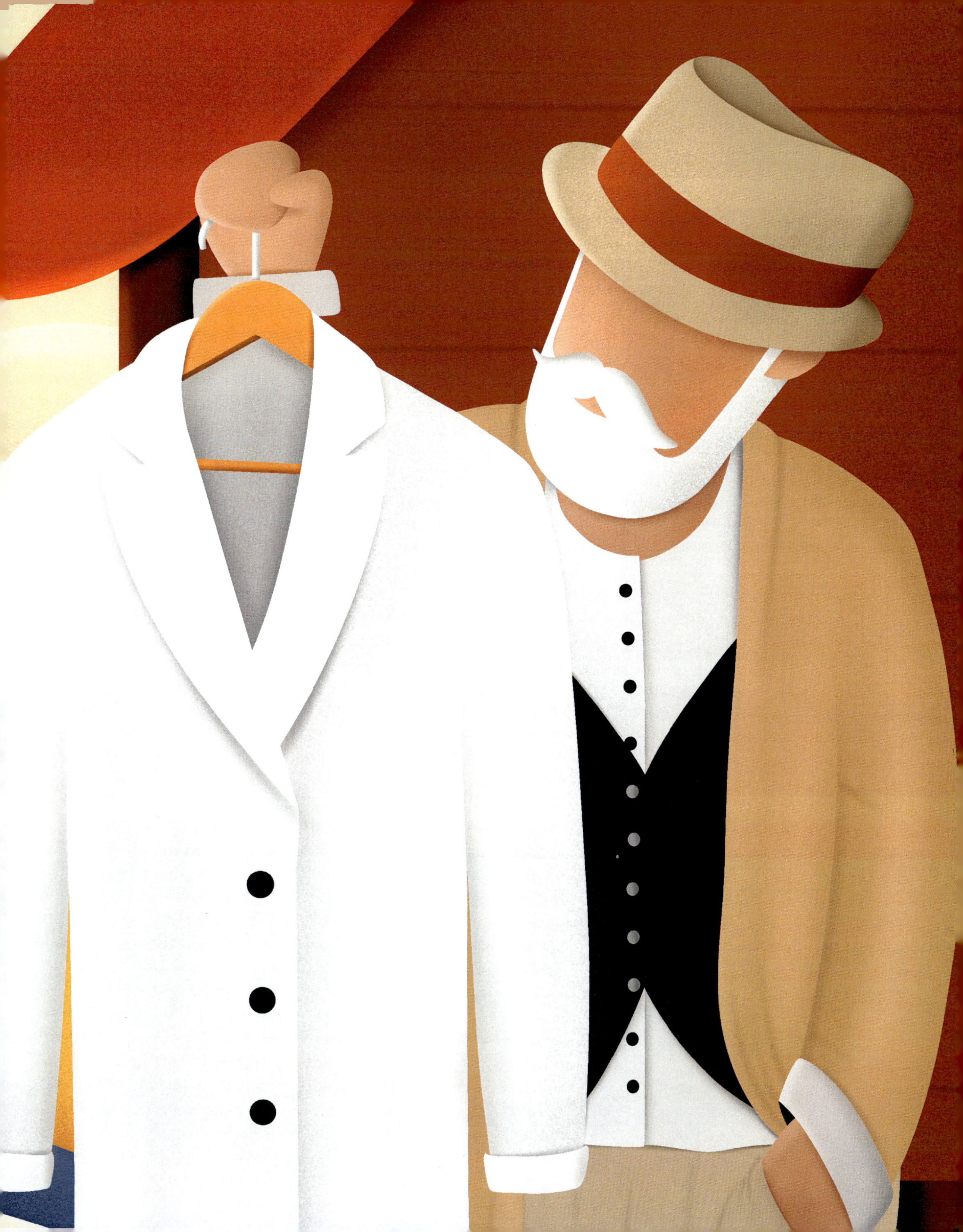

I brought it to the doctor,
Who looked up in delight.
Her old coat was worn
And no longer quite right.

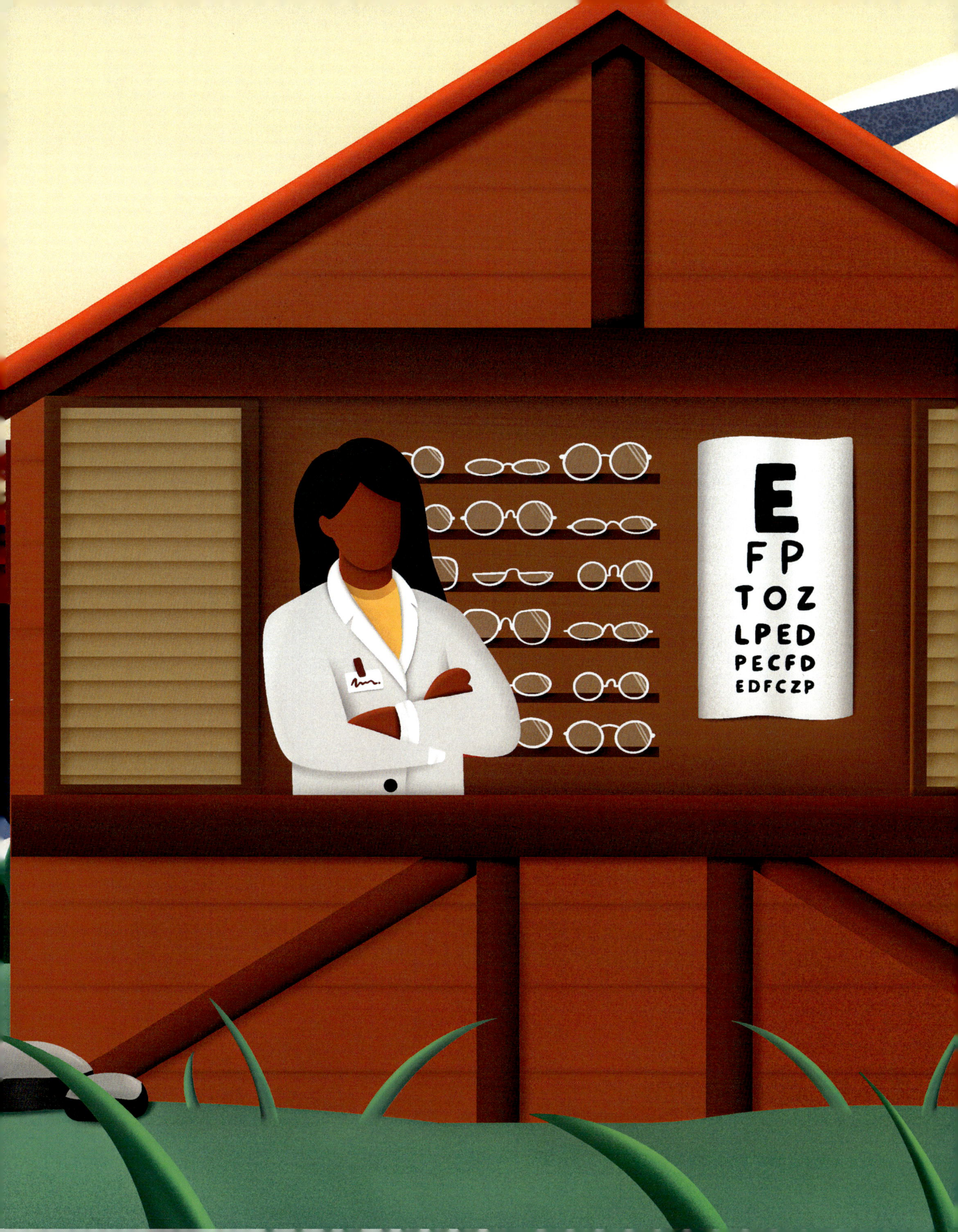
E
FP
TOZ
LPED
PECFD
EDFCZP

"A new coat for my work,
Just what I need!"
She handed me glasses,
A thank-you for my deed.

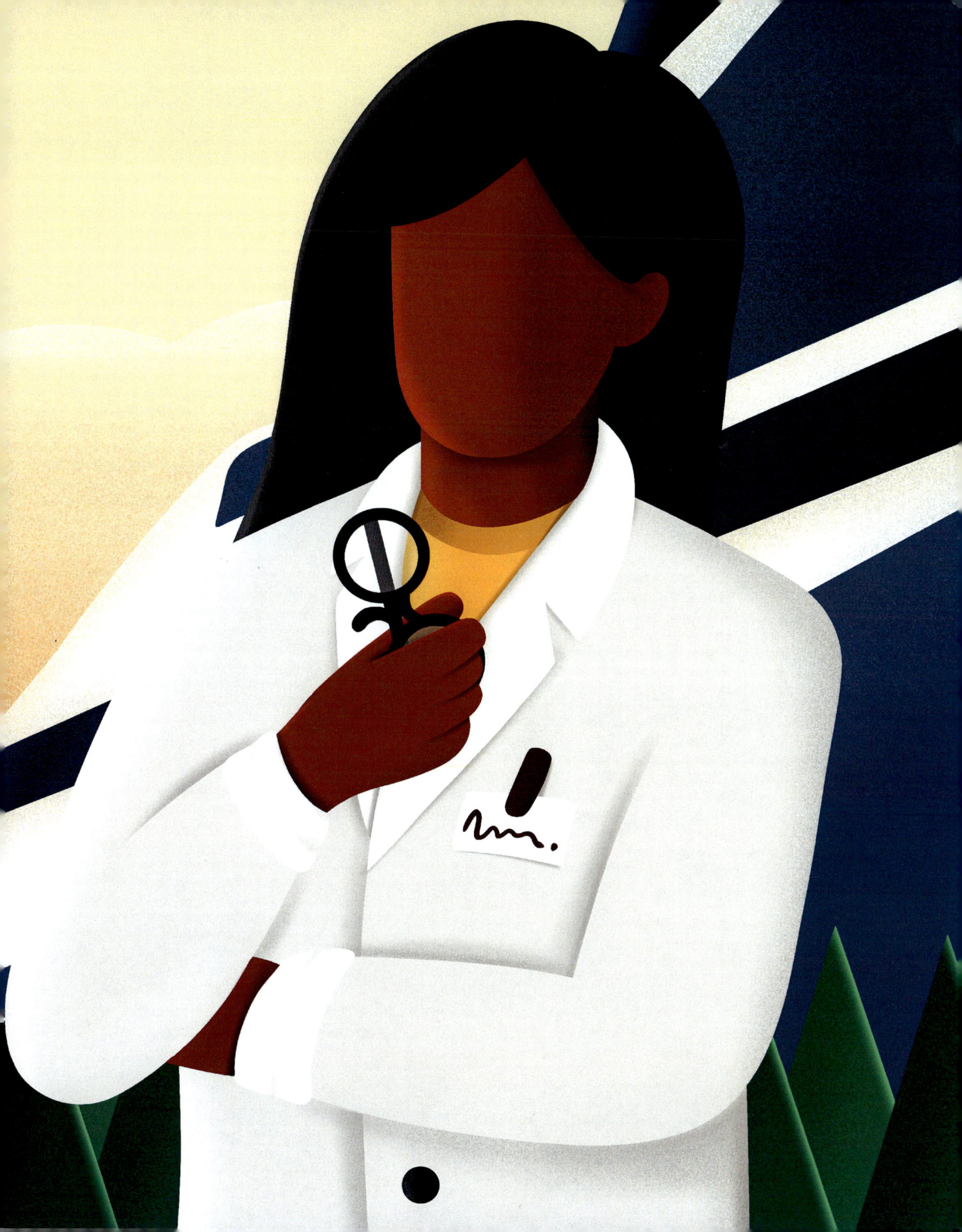

The glasses I gave
To my father, who said…

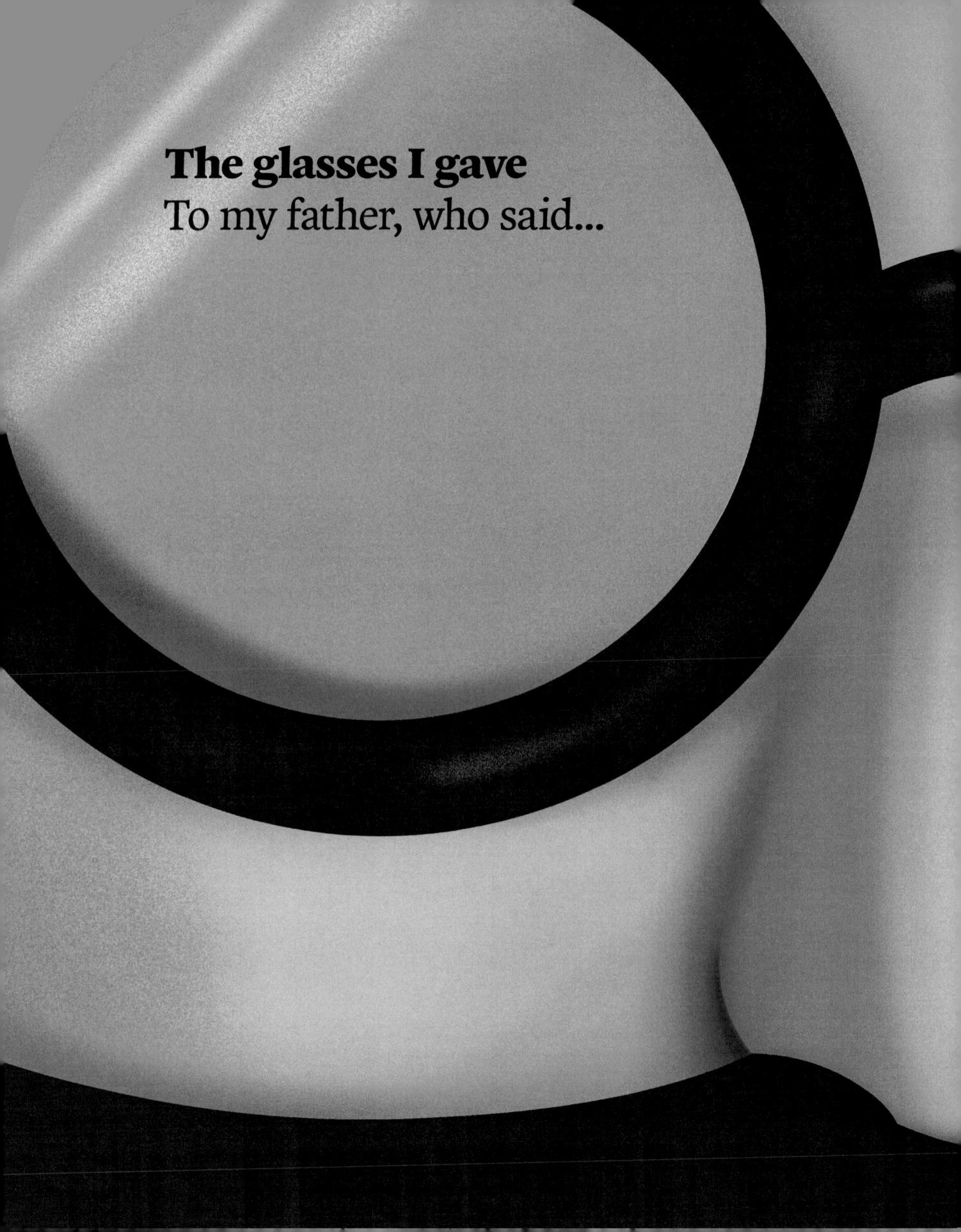

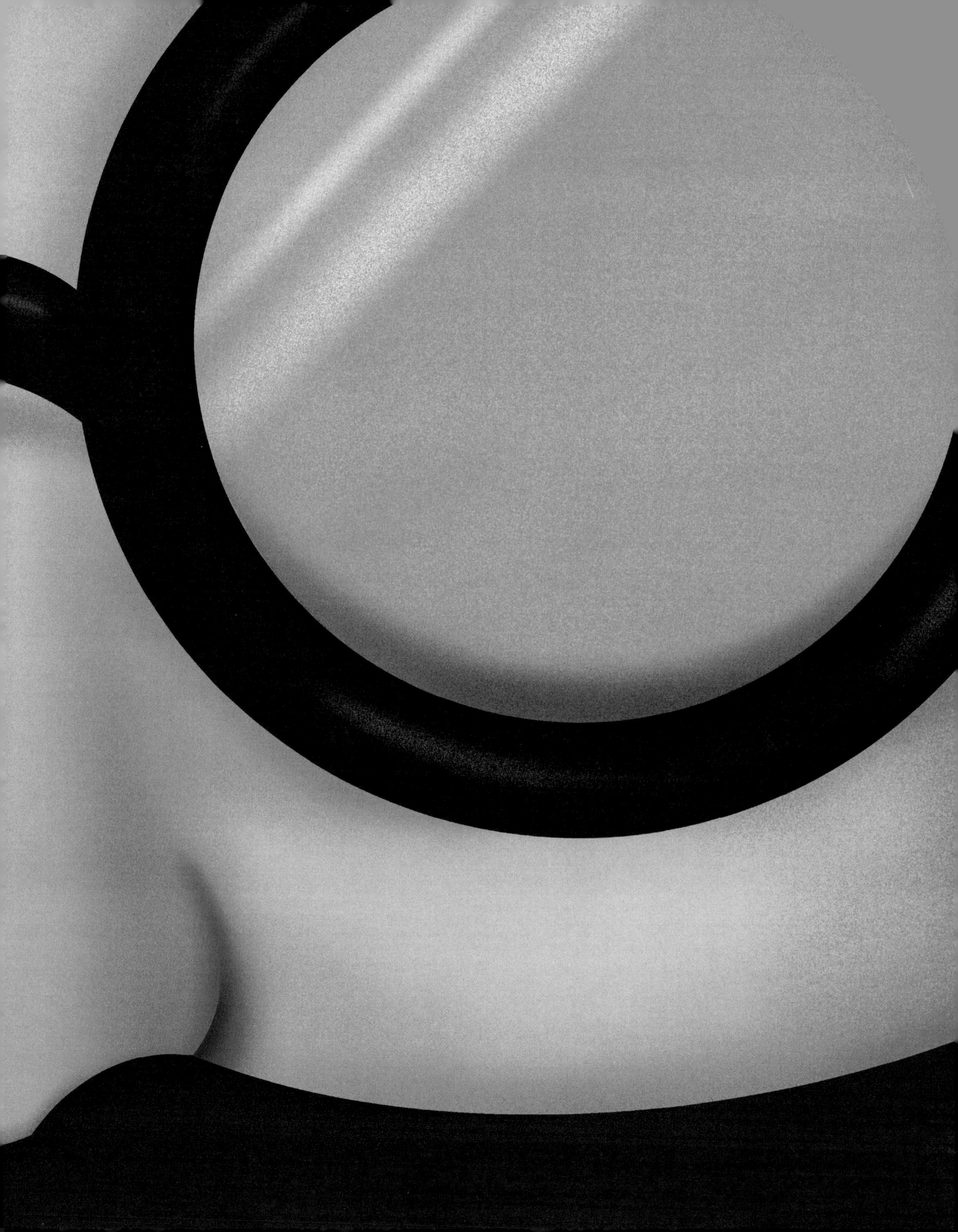

"Now that I can better see,
Let's build something together,
Up high in a tree!"

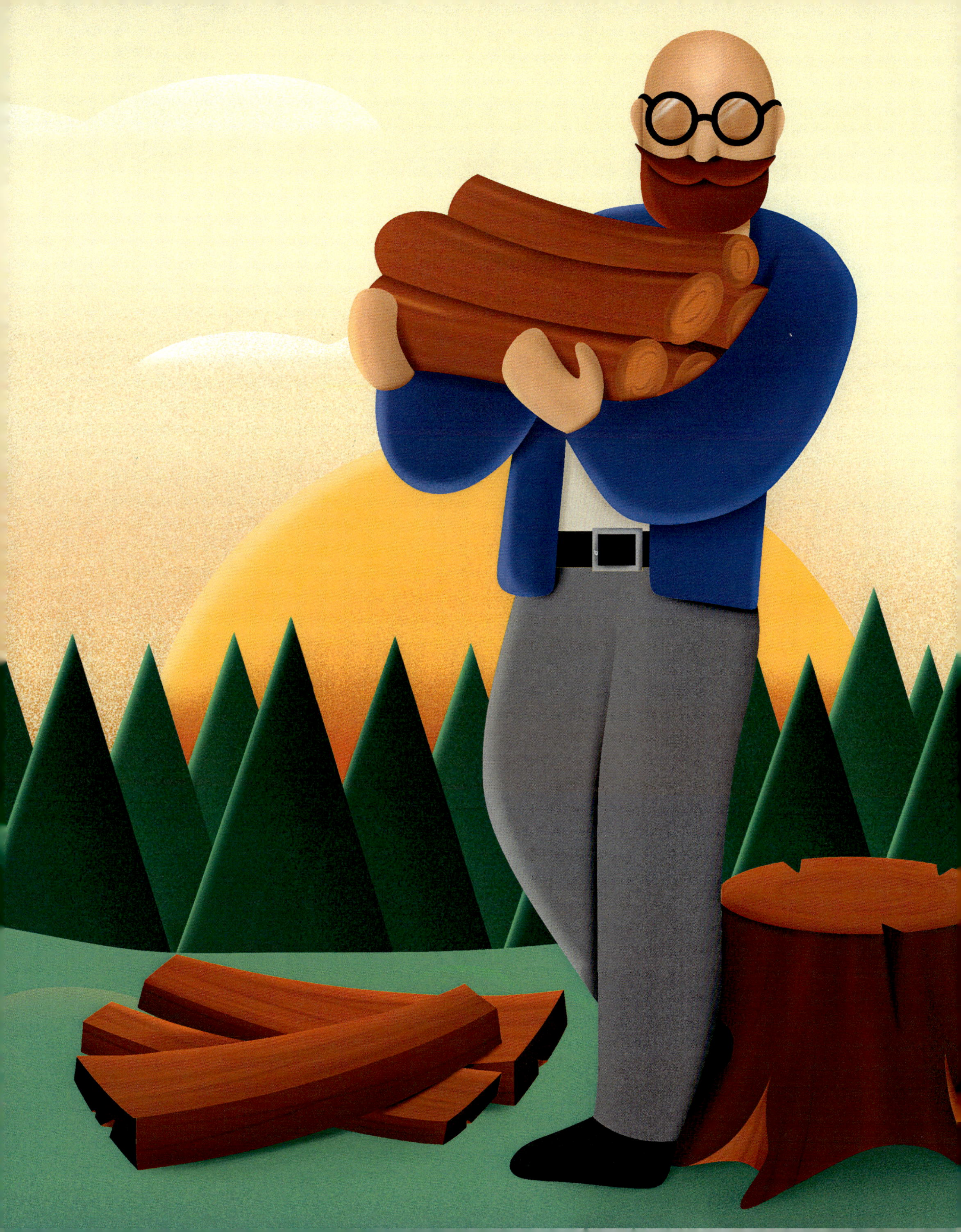

We built a treehouse,
Cozy and high,
With a rope to swing
And a view of the sky.

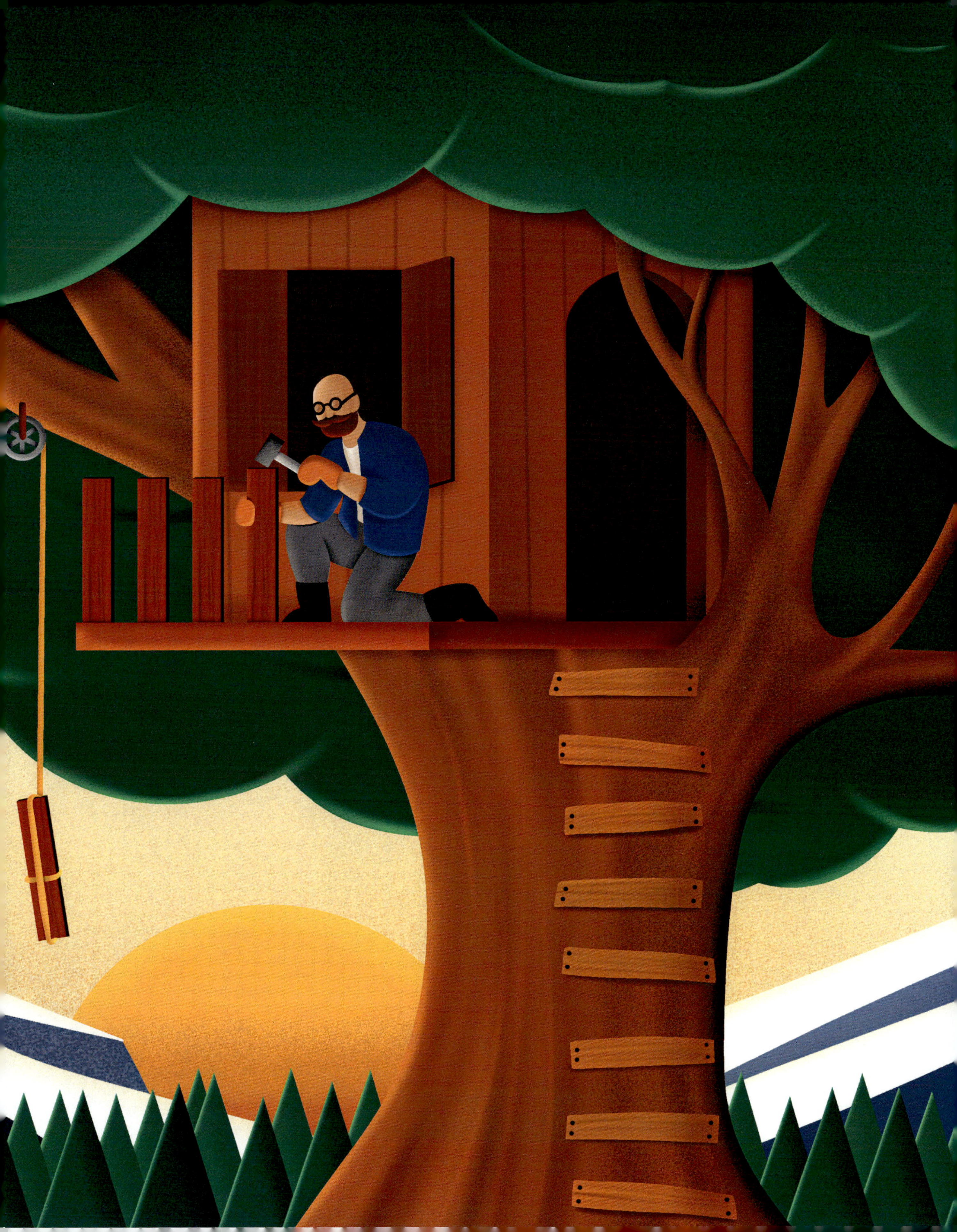

After all that hard work,
We sat on the floor.
We opened a book,
An adventure to explore.

But slowly my eyes started to close,
And then I began to snore.

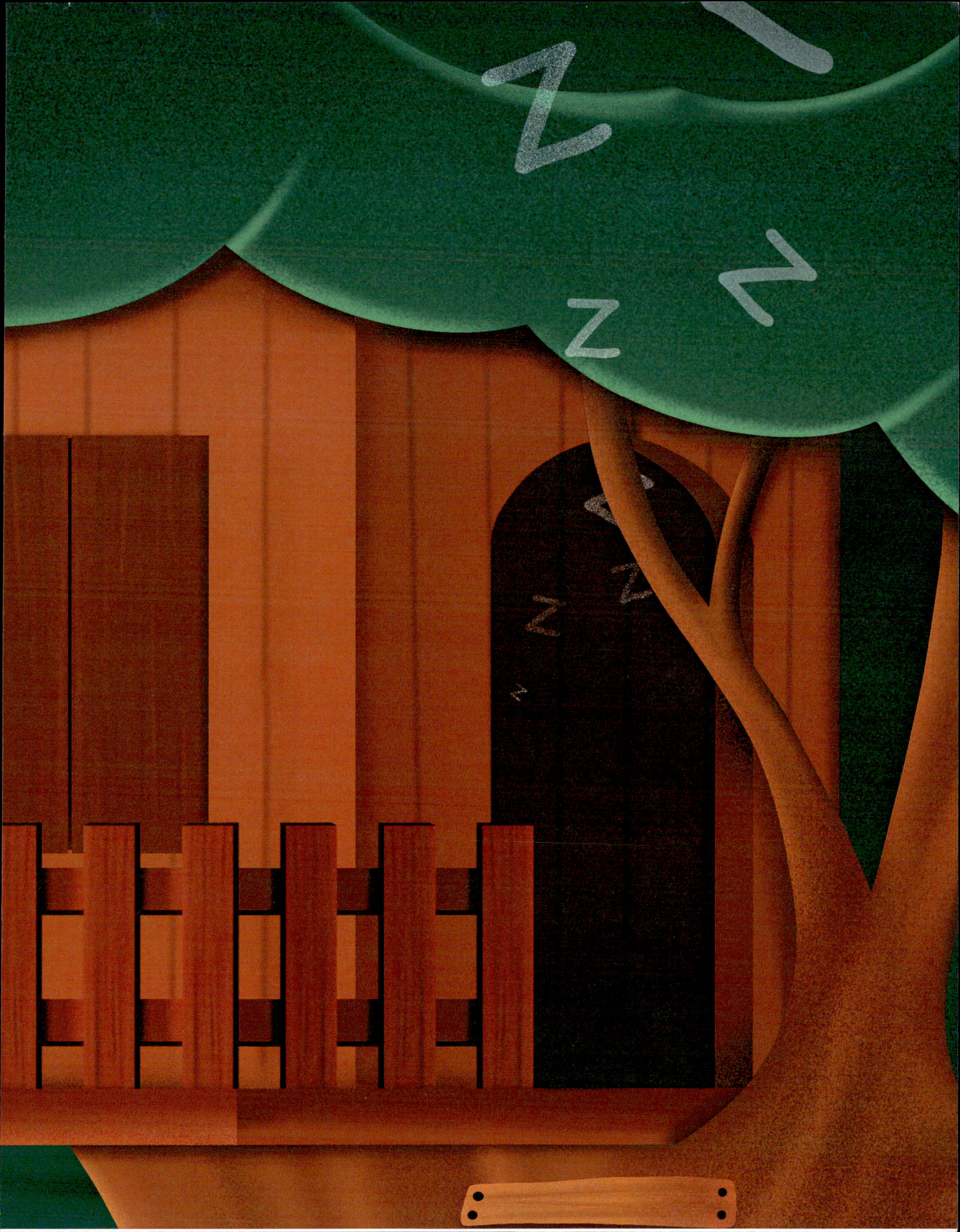

I started the day
With hope and a plan.
To use what I had
And do what I can.

With quick thinking
And a clever mind,
I thought ahead
And left doubt behind.

With every step,
I built my way.
One small choice
Made a brighter day.

THE END.

Copyright © 2025 Siamak Taghaddos.
All rights reserved.

Illustrations by Amélie Touchet.
Poetti Publishing.

New York, NY

poettibooks.com

No part of this publication may be reproduced, stored in a retrieval system or transmitted, in any form or by any means, electronic, mechanical, photocopying, recording or otherwise, without permission in writing from the publisher.

ISBN 978-1-7342464-8-3
Second Edition

FOR CY

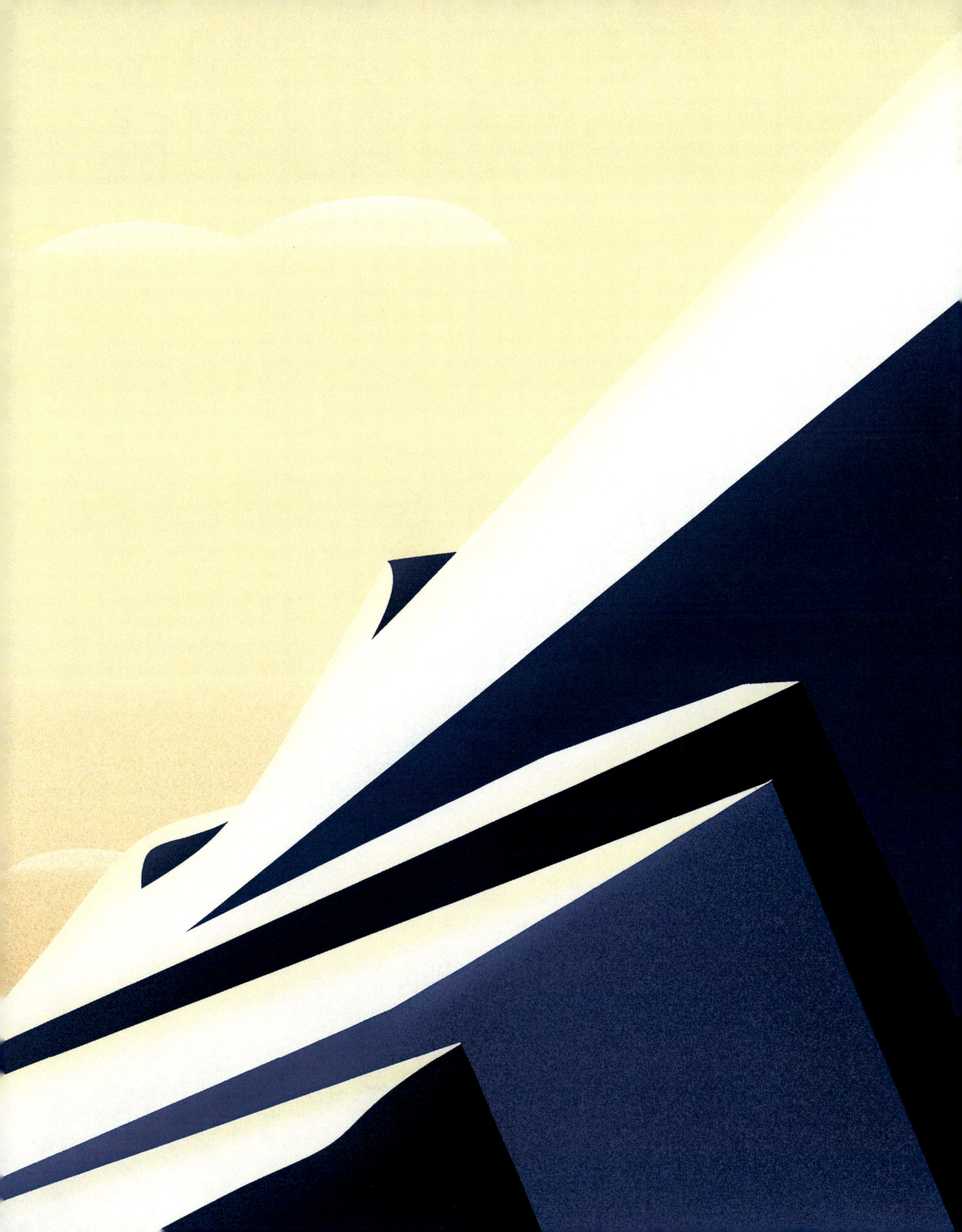

Made in United States
North Haven, CT
09 June 2025